Boogie-woogie Ganesha

by Nishita Chaitanya

C·H·I·N·M·A·Y·A B·A·L·A K·A·T·H·A

One day Ganesha
decided to come down
from Mount Kailash.

He came to earth and joined the family of
Sage Kashyapa and his wife Aditi. He called them
father and mother, and lived as their son.

Delightful, cuddly,
gorgeous Ganesha
had come to earth.

Aditi adored her lovely little baby, and spent all her time with him.

She fed him yummy food, played fun games with him, and told him countless stories. Together they smiled, and giggled, and laughed.

One day Aditi took Ganesha to the river. She always wanted to and so she did.

The very little, very cute, very sweet Ganesha sat on the river bank.

Little Ganesha was enjoying the warm sunlight and the bright blue sky.
He was playing with the soft, fresh grass and tried to catch the colourful butterflies fluttering around.

Just then, little Ganesha heard
Mother Aditi's voice.
He looked down and saw that
his mum was already in the water.

He stretched out his chubby little hands. He wanted to be with his mum. He kept jumping forward as he stretched out further and further until,

The water was refreshingly cool.
Splish, splash, splosh!
Little Ganesha hit his chubby little
hands on the cool clean water.

The water droplets sparkled in the sun,
and danced in the air, and sprayed his face.
This was fun! Lots of fun!

He jumped and dipped. He swayed and he swam. He even tried to splash his mum.

Together they smiled, and giggled, and laughed. Wheeee! So much fun!

But then . . .
something terrible, something very horrible was about to happen.

From under the water came
a crocodile. A very big, long,
dark and scary crocodile.
The crocodile saw chubby
little Ganesha and wanted to
touch him.

The big, long crocodile opened his gigantic, sharp-toothed mouth.

Snap!

Quickly and suddenly, he caught Ganesha.

Ganesha struggled and pushed, he tried to get away, but the crocodile was too big and too strong. The crocodile held onto Ganesha, tightly.

"No! Oh, no!" Aditi cried.
"No! NOOOO!"
Aditi screamed even louder,
"Somebody help! Anybody help!!"

She looked around and called out again,
"Somebody come quickly!
Somebody save my baby!
Please, save him quickly!!"

She rushed over to try and free Ganesha.
She reached out to catch his chubby little hands.

But every time she got closer, the crocodile dragged Ganesha further into the water. Aditi tried harder, reaching out farther. "Ganesha, my baby, hold on . . !"

But the crocodile kept taking Ganesha deeper and deeper into the water.

The people on the banks of the river wanted to help.
Some of them shouted, "Ganesha, hold on!"

Some of them jumped into the river. Some called out to other people to come and help.

But no one was able to free Ganesha from the powerful clutch of the crocodile.

Then, suddenly, there was a twinkle
in Ganesha's bright and beautiful eyes.
He pushed hard against the crocodile
with all his might. And like a flash
of lightning, daring little Ganesha
somersaulted and landed
on the crocodile's back!

Everybody was stunned.
Everybody was amazed.

And then, fearless little Ganesha
did the most surprising thing of all . . .

He started dancing. Ganesha danced from the top of the crocodile's nose to the tip of its tail.

He tapped, and he clapped, and he hopped, and he bopped.

Dhoom! Chak-Chak! Dhoom!
Chak-a-dhoom!

Ganesha giggled
and gurgled
with laughter.

Then he jumped back
into the water, grabbed
the crocodile by its tail,
swung it round and round
and flung it onto the river
bank.

The crocodile landed
with such a **big** thump,
he got a **big** bump!

OUUUCH!

And then . . . it disappeared!

All the people cheered,
"Ganpati Bapaa MORIA! Mangal Moorti MORIA!"

"Yay, Ganesha is unbeatable!"
"The danger is gone.
Ganesha is victorious.
"Ganesha defeated the dangerous
crocodile, so now we're all safe."
"Yes, he removes all our troubles."

Now a tall, handsome man was standing
where the crocodile had been.

He stood with his hands folded,
then bent low, and touched
Ganesha's feet.

"My name is Chitra," he said.
"I was cursed to live as a crocodile,
but now you have saved me.
You have set me free.

"Thank you, kind Ganesha. Thank you
from the top of my nose to the tip of my tail,
and thank you from my head to my toe."

"I had made a mistake," said Chitra.
"I did something very wrong. But then
I was sorry. So very, very sorry.

"Because I said I was sorry, the wise
Sage Bhrigu changed the curse.
He said I would stop being a crocodile
when I was touched by the delightful,
cuddly, gorgeous Ganesha."

"So when you touched me, Ganesha,
I was cured.
"Just your touch, just the sight of you,
cures us all!"

"I was sad that I had made a mistake. But now I think making mistakes is not so bad after all. If you learn your lesson, something good can come from them, too.

"I am so lucky," said Chitra. "I got to see you, o kind Ganesha. I am really, truly lucky, the luckiest of all. The lovable little Ganesha danced on my back!"

Lovable little Ganesha
likes to dance.

Do you?

Where will you let him dance
when he comes to visit you?

Let him dance on your tongue.
Let him dance in your eyes.
Let him dance on your head.
Let him dance through your ears.

Let him dance all the way into your heart, where he can stomp out those yuckky-ickky bits.

Let him smile, and giggle, and laugh. And of course, dance!!

Quickly, tell him to come and dance in your heart.

Well? Have you called him yet?